PLAYDATE PALS

Squirrel is
SAD

Rosie Greening • Dawn Machell

make
believe
ideas

Squirrel's favorite toy was a small brown bear.

His name was Ted.

Squirrel took Ted everywhere:

on walks . . .

up trees . . .

and even in the bath!

Everything was **fun** when Ted was there too.

One day **Squirrel** wanted to play with Ted.

She searched

and searched,

but she couldn't find Ted anywhere!

Squirrel got a **strange**, **sinking** feeling in her tummy.

"Where's Ted?" she **whispered** in a tiny voice.

Everything was **different** without Ted:

walks were **lonely** . . .

climbing trees was **boring** . . .

and baths were **no fun**!

Squirrel didn't feel like **doing anything** without Ted.

That night, there was a **Ted-shaped space** in **Squirrel's** bed.

She felt **lonely** and couldn't sleep, so she **curled** up in a ball and **hugged** her knees.

The next day all the animals were playing together.

Puppy said, "Let's make a den for our favorite toys!"

Squirrel thought about her favorite toy and burst into **tears**.

She **missed** Ted.

Alligator saw **Squirrel** looking **sad**.

He said, "Let's make a Lost and Found poster for Ted. Then if someone finds Ted, he or she can give Ted back to you!"

Squirrel thought that was a great idea.

Squirrel drew Ted on a big piece of paper.
Alligator wrote "Lost Bear" at the top.

Then they put the poster up on the wall.

When Kitten saw the poster,
she said, "I've seen that bear!"

lost bear

She took **Squirrel** to the dress-up box.

Ted was inside!

Squirrel thanked Kitten and Alligator, and then she gave Ted a big **hug**.

She felt **happy** to have such **helpful** friends, and she didn't feel **sad** anymore!

READING TOGETHER

Playdate Pals have been written for parents, caregivers, and teachers to share with young children who are beginning to explore the feelings they have about themselves and the world around them.

Each story is intended as a springboard to emotional discovery and can be used to gently promote further discussion around the feeling or behavioral topic featured in the book.

Squirrel is Sad is designed to help children recognize their own feelings of sadness and how they behave when they are upset. Once you have read the story together, go back and talk about any experiences the children might share with Squirrel. Practice talking about your feelings together and encourage children to do so in other trusted relationships.

Look at the pictures

Talk about the characters. Are they smiling, frowning, or crying?
Help children think about what people look like or how they
move their bodies when they are sad.

Words in bold

Throughout each story there are words highlighted in bold type. These
words specify either the **character's name** or useful words and phrases
relating to feeling **sad**. You may wish to put emphasis on these words
or use them as reminders for parts of the story you can return to and discuss.

Questions you can ask

To prompt further exploration of this feeling, you could try
asking children some of the following questions:

- What makes you feel sad and how do you show it?
- What is the opposite of feeling sad? What can you
  tell me about this feeling?
- When you are sad, what does it feel
  like in your body?
- Can you make a sad face?